Lisa

L   I   S   A

and her soundless world

by Edna S. Levine

illustrated by Gloria Kamen

This book is lovingly dedicated
to children with impaired hearing
and also to Boyce Williams.

Original hardcover edition ©1974
Paperback edition ©1984 by Human Sciences Press, Inc.

Library of Congress Cataloging in Publication Data
Levine, Edna (Simon)
  Lisa and her soundless world.

  SUMMARY: A little girl with impaired hearing learns
through various methods to use and understand speech.

  1. Children, Deaf—Juvenile literature. [1. Deaf]
I. Title.
HV2380.L39   362.7'8'42   73-14819

Library of Congress Catalog Number 73-14819

ISBN 0-87705-104-6   Cloth
ISBN 0-89885-204-8   Paper

Do you remember when you were very small and your mother would tell you about your eyes and your ears and your nose and your mouth? She would tell you:

These are your eyes. Your eyes are for seeing.

And here are your ears. Your ears are for hearing.

This is your nose. Your nose is for smelling.

And here is your mouth. Your mouth is for eating and tasting and talking.

And then mother would give you a little touch on your eyes and your ears and your nose and your mouth. And maybe she would give you a little kiss too.

And then you wanted to see if mother was right. So you closed your eyes. You closed them tight, tight, tight. And what happened?

You couldn't see! You couldn't see anything at all!

And then you pressed your hands over your ears. You pressed them very tight. And what happened?

You couldn't hear! The sounds were all gone!

And then you closed your mouth tight, tight, tight. And you couldn't taste, you couldn't eat, you couldn't talk!

And when you pinched your nose between your fingers, what happened?

You couldn't smell a thing. It was the same as the time you had a bad cold. Your nose was stuffed up. You couldn't smell anything at all!

So you knew that mother was right.

When you opened your eyes again, you saw all the things around you. You saw the people. You saw the street and the cars and the beautiful sky. If you wanted, you could see movies and television and books and pictures. You could see all the things there are to see. Because you had eyes.

And when you took your hands away from your ears, you could hear. You could hear mother laughing and father talking and the music playing on the radio. You could hear the clock ticking and the telephone ringing and the door slamming. You could hear the dog barking. You could even hear your own self telling him to keep quiet. You could hear all the things there are to hear. Because you had ears.

And when you stopped pinching your nose, you could smell all the things there were to smell. You smelled the dinner cooking in the kitchen. You could smell the flowers on the table. You could smell all kinds of things. Why? Because you had a nose.

And when you took your hands away from your mouth, you could laugh and talk and eat and drink. Mother gave you some cookies and milk which tasted wonderful. You said "Yummy!" So, you ate and drank and tasted the delicious cookies and you talked. And all because you had a mouth.

And then you thought to yourself "How lucky I am!
I can see with my eyes.
I can hear with my ears.
I can smell with my nose.
I can talk and eat and drink and taste with my mouth.
I can walk and run and jump with my legs.
I can reach and wave and hug with my arms.
How lucky I am!". . . and you were right.

But—there are children who are not as lucky as you. One of them is Lisa. Lisa is a very pretty girl. She has brown hair and big brown eyes and a pretty smile. Lisa just had a birthday party. She is eight years old and a very happy girl.

But Lisa was not always happy.

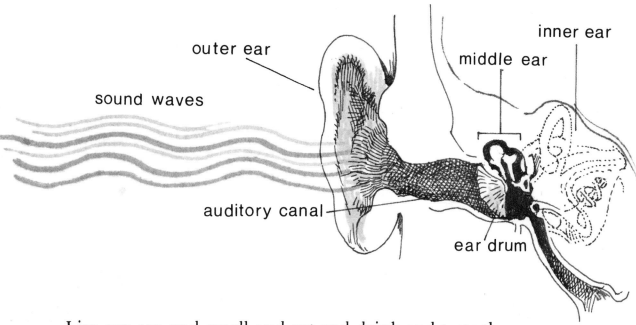

Lisa can see and smell and eat and drink and taste the same as you. But Lisa cannot hear with her ears the same as you. So for a long time she was not a happy girl.

When Lisa was born, she was a beautiful baby. She laughed and cried and played just like other babies. But there was something wrong with the part of her ears that makes us hear. So Lisa could not hear. But nobody knew this. Because nobody can *see* hearing. And nobody can see the part of the ear that makes us hear. It is deep inside our heads.

When Lisa started to grow up, she could not hear her mother laugh or her father talk. She could not hear the doorbell, or the radio, or her kitten, or the children playing in the street. She could not even hear her own self laughing or crying. She could not hear any of the things that you could hear when you were little.

When Lisa grew up some more, her parents began to worry about her. When they talked to Lisa, she would only look at them. She did not say anything. Lisa could not hear what they were saying. So how could she understand them? She did not know what they were telling her. Lisa did not know what anybody was telling her.

Do you want to know how it feels to be like Lisa? Not to know what people are saying to you? Not to hear them?

Go over to the television set and turn it on to your favorite program. Then turn off the sound.

What happens?

You can see the program fine. But you can't hear anything. So you don't know what the people are saying. You don't know why they are laughing. You don't know what they are telling you.

Everything is all mixed up.

But when you turn on the sound again, everything is all right. You know what the people are saying. You know why they are laughing. You know what they are telling you. You know what the program is all about. You *understand.* Because you can hear.

And that is what it is like not to hear. It is like television with the sound turned off. You can turn the sound on again whenever you want to. But nobody could turn on Lisa's hearing. Lisa lived in a soundless world. And because she did, Lisa could not talk.

Lisa could not talk because she could not hear words. Children who hear know what words are because they hear them all the time. But Lisa never heard how words sound, so she did not know what words were. Lisa could not even hear people say her own name: "Lisa." She did not know how her own name sounded!

When Lisa wanted something, she had to *show* what she wanted. She had to point to what she wanted or pull her parents there; or act things out. She didn't know the words to use or how to say them.

Lisa wanted to have friends and play games and have fun, just like you. But none of the children would play with her because she could not talk. When her mother took her to their birthday parties, they would not play with her.

Some children even made fun of her. They called her silly names. They teased her and made her cry.

After a while, Lisa would not go to parties. She didn't want to go anywhere. She thought that nobody loved her.

But she was wrong.

Lisa's mother and father loved her very much. They worried because she did not talk or have friends or laugh. They still did not know that Lisa could not hear. She looked just like other girls, so how could they know that something was wrong? But after a while they took her to the doctor to find out why Lisa did not talk.

The doctor examined Lisa. Then he told her parents that Lisa could not hear. That was why she did not talk. He told them that Lisa was "deaf." "Deaf" means not hearing very well or not hearing at all. So does "hearing-impaired."

Lisa's parents wanted to know what they should do. They wanted to know how to make Lisa hear, what medicine to give her, which hospital could fix her hearing.

The doctor told them that there was no medicine or hospital that could fix her hearing. But when Lisa's parents looked sad, the doctor told them some good news. He told them that there are many ways to help children like Lisa.

Here are some of the ways.

First, Lisa learned about a hearing aid.

What is a hearing aid?

It is like a tiny radio that children who have trouble hearing wear under their clothes, usually on their chests. Sounds go into this little box through a microphone and are made much louder. Then the sounds go along wires to earpieces that the children wear in their ears. And that is the way they hear.

Lisa's parents bought her a hearing aid.

The first time Lisa put it on she jumped for joy. She could *HEAR!* She could hear things she never heard before. She could even hear herself laugh!

Lisa wanted to hear all the sounds there are to hear. To do this, she had to learn how to *listen* with her hearing aid. She had to learn which sounds came from which things. The more Lisa listened, the more she was able to hear. A hearing aid does not help all deaf people. But it helped Lisa. Now she wears one in each ear.

But even a hearing aid can't make Lisa hear as well as other people. She hears people's voices. But she can't make out all the words they are saying. And all the other sounds will never be as loud and clear for Lisa as for people who hear. Even so, it is much better than not hearing at all. So Lisa is very happy with her hearing aid.

But Lisa still did not know about words and talking.

Most children learn words by hearing how they sound. A small child hears her mother say, "Say *Mommy*; say *Mommy*." The child listens and listens, and after a while tries to say "Mommy" herself. She hears her mother say the word, and hears herself say the word. And that is the way that all children learn the words they say—by *first* hearing them.

If you can't hear words, you can't know what they mean or how to say them. There are special schools and hearing and speech centers, though, to help children who cannot hear learn about words and talking. Lisa went to such a school.

Lisa learned many things at the school that most children do not know!

Do you know you can *see* words—not words in books or in writing, but words that people are *saying*? You can see them on people's lips!

Lips move in a different way for many words we say —not all, but many. If you watch carefully, you can tell what the word is by the way the lips move. We call this "lip-reading" or "speech-reading."

Lisa is learning about lip-reading and how to do it. She watches the lips and face of the person who is talking. She tries to understand what the person is saying from the way his lips move. Lisa is learning to *see* what people say.

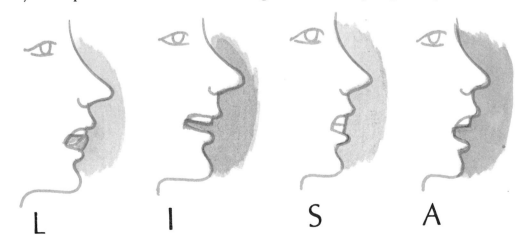

L   I   S   A

To use eyes for ears is a very hard thing to do. Many words look the same on the lips. It is hard to tell them apart. Many people do not talk carefully, so it is hard to see what they are saying. And there are many words that Lisa cannot lip-read because she does not know what they mean. But again, Lisa is very lucky because she is good at lip-reading.

Do you think you would be a good lip-reader? Try and see. Ask your mother or a friend to say your name, but tell them not to say it out loud. When they say your name without sound, you will see how it looks on the lips. You will be lip-reading! Try it with other words too.

When Lisa grows up, she will be able to lip-read many of the words that you are able to hear. Lisa uses her lip-reading the way you use your hearing: to *understand* what people say to her.

Lisa must also learn to talk. When people talk to her, she must be able to answer them. This is very hard to do when you can't hear how words sound.

But Lisa learned that you can *feel* words!

When you say a word out loud, it makes a funny little tingle in your face or nose or throat. We call this "vibration." Try to see for yourself. Put your hands on your throat and say "Go" and feel the tingle it makes, or say "Mommy" and feel the tingle on the side of your nose. Different words make different tingles in different places.

One of the things that Lisa does when she is learning to say a word is to put her hands on her teacher's face or throat or nose. When the teacher says a word, Lisa feels the tingles it makes. Then she tries to get the same tingles herself when she says the word.

But feeling the tingles is only one of the things that Lisa does when she is learning to talk. She also has to watch her teacher's face and mouth and lips to see how the word looks when her teacher says it. She listens with her hearing aid to hear as much as she can of how the word sounds. And finally she puts all these things together and tries to say the word herself. She says it over and over again until the teacher tells her she is saying it right. Lisa can't hear herself very well, so the teacher must tell her when she is saying it right.

This is a very hard way to have to learn to talk, and not all of Lisa's deaf friends are able to do it. Even when Lisa talks, it does not sound the same as when a hearing person talks. This is because Lisa has to learn to talk by *seeing* and *feeling*. Most people learn to talk just by hearing how other people talk and how they sound themselves. Sometimes it is hard to understand what Lisa says.

But Lisa's speech will get better all the time. When it gets to be very good, everyone will be able to understand her. Again, Lisa is very lucky. She has some very smart deaf friends who are very hard to understand.

Some deaf children and many deaf grown-ups know another way to talk. They know how to talk on their hands. It is like making pictures with your hands of what you want to say. We call this kind of talking "sign language." It can be a beautiful way to talk. Almost all grown-up deaf people and many deaf children know the sign language. They also know how to spell out words on their fingers. Every letter of the alphabet has its own finger position. We call this kind of language "finger-spelling." Lisa knows some of these ways of talking, too. She uses them with her deaf friends who can't lip-read very well.

Now that Lisa is eight years old, she is learning to read and write all the words she talks and lip-reads, and many more. She is learning arithmetic too. She will learn all the other things that children learn in regular schools. Maybe she will learn enough to go to one of these schools too one day.

It will take Lisa longer to learn all these things than it takes children who can hear. That is because Lisa must work much harder. But Lisa is smart and she will catch up. Not all deaf children are as lucky as Lisa. They are just as smart, but it is too hard for them to catch up.

Lisa thinks about what she will be when she grows up. She thinks about being a librarian or a model or an artist. She often thinks about being a teacher. She remembers all her deaf friends who are as smart as she is but who have trouble learning to talk and to read and to lip-read. She would like to help such children. She would like them to be proud of themselves and their parents to be proud of them. Lisa's parents are very proud of Lisa.

Lisa is a joyful girl now. She is thinking to herself:
"How happy I am!
I can hear with my hearing aid.
I can lip-read with my eyes.
I can talk with my mouth.
I can talk on my hands.
I can play with my friends—those who hear
　　and those who do not.
And I can love with my heart people everywhere
　　who try to understand my soundless world."

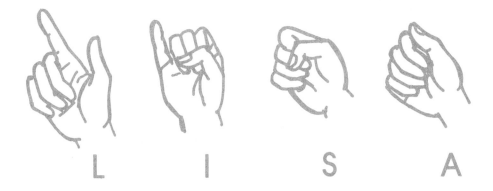

L　　I　　S　　A